A Line Drawn or Printed

Six routes through Madrid

Jayne Marshall

A Modern Odyssey Book

For Aunty Pauline, with all my love, always.

*Mis pasos en esta calle / resuenan / en otra calle / donde /
oigo mis pasos / pasar en esta calle / donde / Sólo es real la niebla*

*My footsteps in this street / echo / in another street / where /
I hear my footsteps / fall in this street / where / Only the mist is real*

Octavio Paz

//

*And this time
It'll take a train to pull me through*

Billy Bragg

Let's make this our departure point. The red dot marking You Are
Here:

> Madrid, 2014. The immense August heat is dry and honest.
> The noise from the street, a continuously breaking wave. A
> hot summer wind lifts the skirt of my red dress; I hurry to
> pin it back down against my pale legs, dropping a shopping
> bag and the postcards I've just bought. A philatelist selling
> his stamps in Plaza Mayor shrugs and smiles: 'Don't worry,
> this is Madrid.'

I arrived in Madrid on little more than a whim, if love can be called
a whim, which let's face it – it definitely can. I moved from the UK
with my older sister, Amy, when we were both in our mid-30s. Apparently, we had reached a point in our lives that necessitated us
burning it all the way to the ground to see what new growth might
materialise in the aftermath. And this, too: I wanted to plot a different course, to know what being a legitimate foreigner would feel like,
versus the outsider on home turf I'd always suspected I was. Moving
was something we planned, though not what came after. Because
that's how life is, isn't it? It throws us into the path of things, often
without our consent or prior knowledge: it journeys us, whether we
want it to or not.

Experiences swirled then collected, eventually coalescing to carve
a path through this new life. I no longer cared if my dress lifted in
the wind; my body adjusted to the climate, I slept on the roof in
the summer and stayed inside if it rained more than a few sad, fat
drops. Themes appeared and grouped themselves together like the

beginning of meaning, or like Octavio Paz listening back to the echo of his own footsteps.

But, before that, another red dot:

I grew up in an in-between space, at the edge of a social housing development on the outskirts of the city of Coventry, a city built on the motor trade. The estate had as its border a long straight road lined with car factories. Beyond the factories ran the train line and beyond that, the start of another housing estate, where my aunty Pauline lived. The train tracks threaded themselves through my childhood. In summer, I would cross back and forth on long cycle rides with my mum and Amy, stopping off at Aunty Pauline's house on the way home for something cool and sweet to drink. If I followed the track left, it would take me into Coventry city centre and if I followed it right, it would take me to Birmingham. As a teenager, my best friend and I would wait on the near side of the station until the bell clanged and the crossing gates began to close, then we'd run under the descending gates to jump the train to Birmingham to go on a shoplifting spree.

Now, moving outwards from that red dot, a line begins to draw itself:

My first job in Madrid was teaching English. My classes were for businesspeople, and I travelled to office blocks all over the city and its outskirts. I got to know the local train network, the Cercanías, like the teaching notes hurriedly written on the back of my hand. Many years later, at a point when I decided it was high time to better myself,

I got a job as an editor and started to use the Cercanías again, for the long commute to the publisher's office outside of the city.

In contrast to the local trains in Coventry, juddering their way between the two housing estates, the Cercanías were tall and sleek, and they glided almost noiselessly into the station. Coming and going, to and from the office, I liked to watch for the spill of the lights as they breached the side of the embankment before the train itself appeared, elegantly navigating the curve. I would step forward to the edge of the platform to watch it arc into the station. It was truly beautiful.

Six years after I moved to Madrid, my aunty Pauline ended her life at the mercy of a train passing through the station I could see from the bedroom window of my childhood home. Here in Madrid, I no longer watch the trains approaching, I don't look for the beam of advancing light, it means something very different now. It means watching her watch her own death approach. Willing it to approach.

Life journeys you, whether you want it to or not — even if you never leave the town where you were born. Though what we do with these unexpected and sometimes startling pivots, and how we allow them to change us, is up for grabs. That's the deal we make: we must accept life's sideswipes in exchange for its gifts. The routes and through-lines of my years in Madrid have been shaped by the train lines that traverse the city, and by those journeys, both wanted and unwanted. And each have weaved themselves in and out of the stories and essays in this book. I hope my footsteps will echo something back to you: a long low whistle in the dark of the tunnel.

ROUTES AND THROUGH-LINES

Bodies
Miniature Precision Components
Saturday's Child
Colour
Redheads
The Blessed Shiver
Leave-taking
A Heartbreakingly Beautiful Setting for Saying Goodbye
Sites of Conscience and Memory
Love
Casio, 1984
If Self Is a Location, So Is Love
Silvia
The City
Forever Falling to The Ground in A Faint
Mi Movida Madrileña
Hello, Sunshine
Others
Baba Ghanoush
Buried in Strange Soil
In a Third Place

A train line runs alongside the outdoor cinema in Parque de la Bombilla. Every 12 minutes, a train passes by, emerging from the huge makeshift screen, or entering it. The low rumble is mostly unobtrusive, the do do do do DO do do *before the next stop announces itself sometimes cuts through and sometimes doesn't, blurring boundaries, realities, adding to the fiction on the screen or pulling me out of it, into another.*

Casio, 1984

We hadn't known each other for very long, so the watch shops served as a proxy, a third person to dampen the intensity of a full day spent together. We wandered from shop to shop, searching for bargains, looking ahead, and talking only when we felt like it. The summer sun was a shock to us too, as — until now — in the couple of months since we met, we had only ever seen one another at night-time. He would show up at my place once he finished work around midnight, and we drank tea, smoked, then made love. By the time the sun rose, I was already on the way to work, having left him sleeping in my bed, the cat curled up in the crook of his long legs.

He didn't drink, though he did smoke. But of his addictions, or dependencies, buying old watches was the most imperative. He spent money he didn't have, projecting onto his purchases dreams of huge future profits via specialist reselling websites, dreams that seemed to me to be very slow in materialising. But it made him happy, the joy of a rare find illuminating his day and, by extension, our excursions. He knew Madrid and her terrain like no one else I knew in the city, having been born there, and never having ventured out. He didn't ever tell me where we were headed, but I was happy to follow him around, down streets I hadn't seen before, and some I had, but now saw as if refracted, lit with light and colour.

The watch shops themselves were rare finds. Like in most capital cities, the small businesses were being displaced by the mirrored echo of chain stores, as well as by technology — time itself working against them. As he questioned and haggled with the shopkeepers it was pleasant to imagine customers coming and going, asking for watch batteries to be changed, wasted straps to be replaced. An act of imagination was necessary, as the shops were always empty. Hopeful, handwritten signs announcing new and unmissable offers yellowed, unread, in the windows.

One shop was called Dimar. A contraction of both the owners' surnames, although only Mar remained now. It was hidden away in an arcade between two busy streets. There were only two other premises still operating, one sold analogue cameras and the other was a sign-writer's workshop, making the whole place otherworldly and a little eerie. Inside Dimar everything was pristine. Watch parts were organised by maker and by year, in four great walls of drawers. He asked for a new strap for a Casio 1984, which was located and fitted in a matter of minutes. Waiting, he scratched at his thigh, which I knew to be red and raw under his jeans. One night, in the dim light of the bedroom, he had seen me looking and had told me it got worse when he was anxious. Above the counter there was a screen with space enough for triple figures, imploring customers to take a ticket and wait their turn. It was switched off.

Each of these trips was also a trip through his past, embedded as it was in the city itself. He showed me the streets where he had played as a kid, where Madrid's first Chinese restaurant had opened its doors, his first apartment, with his first girlfriend. One day we came upon a building that had been almost completely demolished, only the façade remained, held up at the back with scaffold poles. He stopped in his tracks, fished his phone from his pocket and took a photo. He told me that his sister had worked there as a teenager, when it had been a large and cavernous bookshop, the name of which he could no longer remember.

I was marking time, too. Looking for signs; quietly taking notes and measuring them against experience. In my last relationship, had I already started to feel lonely after four months? Was I miserable by our six-month anniversary? I counted eight months before I had been told: 'I love you, but...'. Now, with him, it was different. Calm. Metronomic. A clock ticking unnoticed in the background. Yet I worried that without the intensity — traumatic, corrosive as it had been, but binding all the same — we would grow bored of one another. What should come after 'I love you', if not a storm of emotions? And what would hold us together if we weren't desperately trying to weather that storm? After hours traipsing the streets of Madrid, however, I was often too tired to keep worrying at it, and so calm descended all the same, without the storm.

One of the watch shops has admitted defeat and is closing down. Everything must go. *Hasta fin de existencias.* It sounded so much more apocalyptic in Spanish, perhaps appropriately so. The shop had been filled with all available stock. The watches were everywhere, neatly lined up in rows in the cabinets and on every other spare surface. None of them were working, each instead commemorating a different, unremembered moment in the shop's history. He asks to take a closer look at one of the watches with a slim face. The green plastic strap is faded and the owner apologises and offers a further discount. How long since anyone handled it? Felt excited at the thought of wearing it. He doesn't buy it and we leave the shop empty-handed. Outside, the sun blazed on. He leans down and kisses me on the top of my head.

I had never owned a watch. I didn't like the heavy sensation on my wrist, neither was knowing the time something I was particularly interested in. No one else in my family had one either. Although, on special occasions, Dad would wear the watch that had belonged to his father. It had been given to my grandfather on his retirement and was incrusted with a Masonic coat of arms. It no longer worked, but that wasn't the point. On his 50th birthday, my sister and I bought Dad a new watch. We engraved it with the date and our names. He cried when we gave it to him. It was only the second time in my life that I had seen him cry and it made me intensely sad. I knew he wasn't crying for the emotion of the moment, moved by the gesture, but because Mum had just left him after 25 years of marriage and — I suppose — he was asking himself a lot of difficult questions; wondering what the next 25 years might look like.

He stops dead in the street. I had been in the middle of a sentence and didn't know I'd lost his attention. My hand still in his, I am yanked back on myself and almost fall, but he doesn't notice, his eyes are fixed on something he has spotted in a shop window. To me it looks like a cumbersome watch from the early noughties, one I remember everyone wanting, which I couldn't understand then and understand even less now. Inside the shop, there are three clocks on the wall, showing the time in Madrid, London and New York. London is five minutes out. It's hot and the owner repeatedly wipes his forehead with a discoloured handkerchief as he laboriously explains each and every function of the watch. He has run out of money so he asks me if I will pay for it and tells me he will give me the cash later. When we leave, he is ecstatic; this is the best find so far. All the money spent, we go back to his apartment. He extracts four 20 euro notes from under his mattress and hands them to me. We lay down on the bed. I bury my face in his curls and we quickly fall asleep. Somewhere a church bell chimes, momentarily returning Madrid to a *pueblo*. A slight breeze from the window cuts through the heat every now and then. When we wake up, it's dark already.

Sites of Conscience and Memory

Madrid's Carabanchel prison was originally built by and for political prisoners after the Franco dictatorship seized power at the end of the Spanish Civil War. It closed in 1998 and was later mostly demolished. The buildings that remain now house a controversial detention centre for undocumented immigrants. It is campaigning to become a Site of Conscience and Memory — a place of memory that confronts both the history of what happened there and its contemporary legacies.

The need to remember often competes with the equally strong pressure to forget.

I've lived in five apartments since I moved to Madrid, so most days I pass by somewhere I used to live. Which is to say: most days I'm forced to consider the legacy of those places – my own personal sites of conscience and memory. Places that I want to both honour and to reconcile what went on within their walls, in order to move forward with greater self-knowledge and dignity.

Plaza de la Paja

The first apartment represented the dream of a life my sister, Amy, and I felt ourselves to be creating after we emigrated. The flat had marble floors, high ceilings and built-in bookcases next to two ornate balconies which overlooked the dusty rhombus of the plaza. The plaza was flanked on one side by a row of bars, and on the other by a convent, whose swaying cypress trees enclosed in a hidden cloister, were just visible from our window. The apartments that we could see from our balcony, stacked one upon the other, were equally ornate and they also represented a legacy, that of the Madrid de los Austrias. So, wherever we looked, in or out: beauty.

The first Sunday, after cleaning and unpacking for hours while listening to everyone else in the city have fun, we called it a day and went out for a walk. A great wave of noise surged up to greet us as we left the apartment building. The plaza was carpeted with a snow of discarded paper napkins from the surrounding tapas bars and a large group of people had gathered to one side, in a sunny triangle, enjoying the last of the early spring warmth. Amy and I stood tentatively at the edge of the fray. I asked a man standing near us if it was a bank holiday. A smile broke across his face, and he replied: 'No. This is normal.'

After a month, we decided to throw a housewarming party. Amy and I didn't know anyone in Madrid, so to make up the numbers we invited whoever dropped us a kind word. We also invited all of our neighbours in the apartment block, buying a bundle of vintage postcards from the flea market to post under their doors as invitations. We agonised over what to write, what words represented us — which us we wanted to represent – and whether or not to use the formal third person, consulting our grammar dictionaries and arguing over the advice.

The party started at ten in the evening and the last guest left at midday the next day. It was loud and hectic, stressful, messy and packed out, and we had a great time. People we didn't know danced across the expensive wool rug that Amy had shipped over from the UK or spilled out onto the balconies, more smiles breaking across new faces.

More than once, Amy and I came across one another hiding in the kitchen, needing a break from speaking Spanish, or perhaps a break from that new life we were tentatively creating. The police gave us a warning for noise. Once at 2 am and again at 5 am. Two of our neighbours came. Sergio was the first to arrive, his friend Santos in tow, and I noticed without noticing the way that Santos looked at my sister.

Calle de la Amnistía

After Santos moved in with Amy, I had to leave the apartment on Plaza de la Paja. My new flat was even more beautiful than the one I had shared with my sister, but it didn't feel like a home and I never wanted to be there, instead spending as much time as possible outside, walking the streets of the unfamiliar city.

For the first two weeks after moving in, I lived amongst the boxes that I didn't have the energy or the desire to unpack and thought about retreating back home to the UK, to my boyfriend of nine years who I'd left behind there, and to a version of myself that I recognised. A return to a life that left all questions appealingly alone, unpicked at and undisturbed, was seductive, so I wrote to a mutual friend telling her what was on my mind. It took her a week to work up the courage to tell me that my boyfriend had a new girlfriend. Like Amy with Santos, he was happily rediscovering the world with someone other than me. Our decisions had been made and there was no reversing it now. And so, I stayed. To see if I was capable of making a life in Madrid alone, or not.

Calle de la Paloma

Cristina, a mutual friend whom Amy and I met around the *barrio* when we first moved, called me out of the blue one day to say she was looking for a housemate. I didn't know her all that well and my tendency towards solitude made me balk at the idea, but I somehow understood it was the right thing to do. As easy as it would have been for me to stay holed up alone in Calle de la Amnistía, I knew at some point I was going to have to break myself loose.

Cristina was a psychologist and her practice occupied a cramped waiting area in the hall and a small room off it. From the bathroom, I could hear the conversations that went on within and often lingered after a shower, listening in. I sometimes heard puzzling vignettes, such as *The problem is her laugh, it's too loud.* But more often, the comments were depressingly mundane. A sort of universal human chorus: *I don't understand... / I want* (but can't have)… The bathroom was also the clients', so occasionally, while eavesdropping, I heard the request to have a toilet break and had to bolt down the hall to my bedroom, leaving ghostly, wet footprints in my wake.

We got on well until I met V and our friendship, for reasons I didn't fully understand, fell apart. The last image I have of Cristina is of her pursuing me down that same hallway the day I arrived to pick up the last of my boxes, shouting accusations about a broken lock, her long brown hair fanning out behind her and her white nightie flapping around her arms, which were raised in outrage at all the bad things I'd done while living in her home, and which I had never before known existed.

Calle de San Isidro Labrador

San Isidro Labrador is the patron saint of Madrid and of agricultural workers. V and the saint shared a birthday, but V hated Madrid and his thinking veered more to the individual than the collective, so that's all they shared. The apartment had almost no windows and faced an internal patio where the only view up or down was of the neighbours' washing. I always worried about our arguments echoing through the patio — all those angry words reverberating up and into their homes.

After we broke up and he moved out, I stayed in the apartment for another year. But I left the light switch that he had punched broken unrepaired as a reminder — a warning to myself. It was in Calle de San Isidro Labrador that I became better acquainted with myself. V taught me many things in an indirect way. Such as: what had compelled me to dredge the sea of his troubled mind, and why it was that I believed I could fix him. Why I thought I loved him more than I loved myself. Later I realised that he had felt familiar in a very deep and intractable way, an echo of something or someone from long ago resounding back to me. I had I looked to him to locate me, to quell that echo, my welfare and my sense of self tied completely up with his own.

He also taught me how to cut the perfect watermelon.

Calle de López Silva

I moved to Calle de López Silva in the middle of the worse snow-storm to descend on the city in 50 years. I dragged my cases, my boxes of books, the cat in his carrier, over icy streets piled up at the edges with snowdrifts. Madrid was utterly unrecognisable. And she stayed that way for two long weeks.

The apartment, at the very top of the building, feels safe and co-coon-like but also gives me a feeling of freedom and expansion; the blue Velázquian sky and the light and the height all combining to lift me upwards — a boat at the crest of a wave. If I lean far enough out of the bedroom window and crane my neck a little, I can see the *sierra*, the mountains that ring Madrid, that keep their snow like the spray of paper napkins from the tapas bars on Plaza de la Paja, even after the rest of us have succumbed to the advancing summer heat.

On Sunday mornings, the sounds from the weekly flea market wake me up. The woman who runs the stall below my window sells tights in winter and bikinis in summer, but her sales pitch is always the same: 'I'm here, take advantage!' As if she weren't always. As if she weren't as reliable as one season following another, as the Sunday market itself, always managing to rise up out of the wild terrain of the city night.

There is a small terrace, so the cat is happy too; he finally has space to roam, as is his nature. At night he disappears into the darkness, exploring the rooftops, not coming home until the thin, blue light of dawn. I like to think of him walking the whole city, roof by roof.

15

The journey to the office was full of anxiety; the suffocating feeling of not being good enough, not knowing what I was doing, seeing myself as awkward and irrevocably, eternally foolish. But I loved the train ride home — the relief at having got through another day, the quiet, the mental exhalation. While the rest of the passengers looked down into other, digital worlds, I looked out of the window at the abandoned Ferris wheel, high up on an embankment; at the house with the empty swimming pool, a plastic chair tucked into a corner of the deep end, where sometimes I would see a man sitting, enjoying the shade it afforded. Every small landmark took me closer to the safety of home. Between two of the stations, there was a row of small, one-story houses with colourful shuttered windows tucked between the offices and the blocks of flats. It flickered by like a mistake.

Forever Falling to The Ground in A Faint

Ben Lerner's *Leaving the Atocha Station* begins like this:

The noise from the Plaza Santa Ana seeps into Adam's dreams, then wakes him. He makes coffee and climbs onto the roof of his attic apartment to drink it. The cover of the Spanish translation of the novel depicts this opening scene —a pair of jeaned legs on a roof, Madrid laid out before the reader. The first-person view of the camera is Adam's view, and so also the view of the reader. But what are we looking at?

The story I want to tell begins like this:

Amy slides the book across the table towards me, her elegant hand flat against the cover, then sits back in her chair. The boat we are on, which is also a bar, rocks a little as another, bigger boat passes alongside it. Or, now I think, maybe it wasn't the boat moving — it was our world shifting, just a little. *Read this.* She says. *Before we go.* I look down at the book. (It's only years later I realise that the colourful lines on the cover coalesce to depict Madrid's local Cercanías trains.) It's a slim volume. I've never even heard of Atocha Station.

In 2013, before we left home to spend a month in Madrid studying Spanish, Amy made a reading list. She thought, instead of a guidebook, we should read novels that had the city at their back. In the end, we only read one book because we fell in love with *Leaving the*

Atocha Station and its examination of the un-everydayness of everyday life in Spain and life in another language, and with its posturing but relatable protagonist, whom we aligned with the author himself. We wanted to be immersed not only in Madrid itself, but also specifically Lerner's Madrid. And so, after arriving, we commenced where the novel does, with the protagonist, Adam, at the Prado. In room 58, less than an hour after waking and climbing down from the roof of his apartment, he positions himself before Roger Van der Weyden's *Descent from the Cross* and awaits equipoise.

In room 58, we stood and looked at the painting, too. Our experience of that work of art filtered through and contingent on the other. We waited until the guard left on his rounds of the other rooms, the crackling sound of his walkie-talkie fading into nothing, and took pictures of each other in front of it. There we were, our heads peeping up from the bottom of the frame, while Van Der Weyden's Mary swooned above us. From the novel we learnt that the blue of her robes are unsurpassed in Flemish painting. After finding our way out of the labyrinthine Prado, we followed Lerner backwards through the opening pages of the novel, up the narrow, leafy Calle de Las Huertas and into the Plaza Santa Ana where we stood gazing up, moving on the spot in a slow circle and trying to guess which had been his apartment when he lived in Madrid, doing whatever it was that Fulbright scholars did, and when the seeds for the novel had been planted.

Like Almodóvar before him, Lerner's Madrid made the city fully real to me; the novel holding something more visceral and broadly true than the city actually and physically before me. It became the supportive narrative to our month. After Spanish class let out in the early afternoon, we investigated a new location referenced in the novel. We went to all the bars in Plaza Chueca, looking for the one with the glittery cushions. We hung out on the terrace at the Círculo de las Bellas Artes, imagining Lerner drinking a crisp white Albariño and fiddling with the 'alien looking' two-euro coin. We tracked down the bar where Adam usually had breakfast and were underwhelmed by the bar itself, which was mainly filled with tourists, but lit up by the thought that we might be eating our *pan con tomate* at the same table as Adam/Lerner had. We researched the exclusive restaurant where Adam has a psychotic episode towards the close of the novel, but didn't eat there because we didn't like the look of the meat-heavy *madrileño* dishes on the menu. We covered everything we could, but kept finding ourselves back in the centre of the Plaza Santa Ana, gazing up and around at the windows of the apartments, moving in an ever-repeating circle and wondering from which rooftop Lerner once gazed down to where we were now looking up.

Eventually, we wrote to him. We found the name of his agent and sent her an email detailing our project and the afternoons spent staring at the apartment buildings on the plaza. We also attached the photos of us in front of *Descent from the Cross*. The next day we had a reply with the address of the flat where Lerner had lived. We skipped our last Spanish class and set out to find it.

We stood for a good long while staring at his front door, with a lot more attention than we had paid in the Prado. A few hours later his agent sent a new email, this time with a photo of Lerner, also in front of *Descent from the Cross*, also chopped off at the neck to make room for the keeling Mary. We sat at one of the aluminium tables of one of the bars on the Plaza Santa Ana, the accordion player plying his trade in the background, and scrolled back and forth through the three photos on Amy's phone: me in the Prado, Amy in the Prado, Ben in the Prado. Every now and then, we looked up at each other and grinned.

There was something about the meaningless, meaningful stalking that allowed us a sense of belonging. Lerner's fictionalised Madrid became our Madrid, letting us inhabit the city on our own terms, at a different, private level. We couldn't ever be native in the real, physical city, but in this other one we could. We were. That odd little exercise became a stake driven into the ground; the first foundation laid for eventually emigrating. And it has remained with me — Lerner's novel, and the moment in the Prado, marking a point at which my life changed forever, held in eternal suspended animation, like Mary, forever falling to the ground in a faint.

Baba Ghanoush

So, anyway, when we descended from our rented hilltop cottage, down to the local village to buy supplies, we'd bought more alcohol than we did food. And it's only now, as we light up the barbeque, that we realise. I stand, staring at the flickering coals — the only light for miles around — a cool glass of light yellow wine in my hand, and in that moment (in which I breathe deeply the non-city air and feel a slight stinging in my shoulders where I had gotten a bit too much sun) I don't really care about food. It was enough to be here.

'Hey, I reckon I can make baba ghanoush with these!'
I turn and see Luca, backlit in the doorway of the cottage, brandishing a huge pair of aubergines. One of the few foodstuffs that had made it back up the hill with us.

'Barbequed baba ghanoush?'
I'm unconvinced.

'Yeah! It's just about our only option anyway.'

'Are you going to add rosemary?'
I ask this with pretended innocence as, since Luca discovered a rosemary bush on the road near the cottage, he had been putting it in everything.

'Uskuti habibti!'
I roll my eyes at him. Even though he can't see me.

'I have to admit, this weird, barbequed baba ghanoush is really tasty.'

'Told you.'

There's a pause, and I know what's coming.

'I miss Jerusalem.'

'I know babe... But, also, you do know you're Italian, don't you? And that you live in Spain now.'

'Yeah… yeah. But I don't feel it. I'm trapped in the wrong nationality.'

'Like this baba ghanoush.'

'Exactly. Just like this... *babaggione.*'

We guffaw. It's a familiar refrain. Familiar to anyone who is from one place, but lives in another. And it draws us closer, as it always does, our friendship having been founded on foreignness.

'Food is probably my only home.'

He says this without artifice, more as if he is just turning the idea over in his head for the first time, going back over his life, charting a course through all the countries and languages he has moved through, taking stock of what had to be left behind and what remained with him. He is suddenly very still and in the dim light I see him staring into the invisible horizon; I feel the dark turn of his thoughts. I ruffle his curls.

'Drink your wine, we have more bottles than we have days here.'

He grins. I propose a toast:

'To aubergines.'

'To aubergines! May they always taste like home.'

'Wherever that is.'

'Whatever that is...'

Getting off the train at Sol, I see my new boss in the distance, on a different part of the platform. I didn't know we shared the same route home, and I keep waiting for her to disappear in some unknown direction, but we ascend the same escalator, we leave by the same exit, we walk down the same street, and the next. I have the feeling I am doing something sinister and prowler-like, and that I should have run and caught her up so we could walk together, but I didn't do that. I don't want to do that. So, instead, I keep following her.

The Blessed Shiver

Madrileños say that the sky above their city is Velázquian blue. It honestly is beautiful, of a blue which is hard to classify, so although I only know *Las Meninas* (which features no sky and no blue to speak of) it feels to me like an appropriate description: something hard to classify describes something else hard to classify. When the sun begins to set, the clouds often turn pink. *My pink sky* is just one of many terms of endearment Nabokov invented to address Véra, which is beautiful and unusual too, in a different way.

Sometimes, on the train on the way to work, as we pull away from the city and head towards the mountains, the sunrise sets the sky alight. Instead of Nabokov's pink or Velázquez's blue, it's all fiery reds and oranges that belong to no-one. People move to the window to take photos. Me included, once or twice. But it never looks the same on my phone as it does through the train window. I've found that it's better to just leave myself within the scene (like Velázquez in his *Las Meninas*).

The impulse to capture — to fix in language or in a photograph — life's more elusive experiences as well as compulsive, can be transcendent. See Nabokov:

A sunset, almost formidable in its splendor, would be lingering in the fully exposed sky … I did not know then (as I know perfectly well now) what to do with such things—how to get rid of them, how to transform them into something that can be turned over to the reader in printed characters to have him cope with the blessed shiver.

Compulsive, transcendent, but hard to pull off. Poetry, said Robert Graves — who must have witnessed many a magnificent and shifting sky from his home in Deià on the coast of Mallorca — is a struggle with 'the huge impossibility of language'.

Probably.

But that won't get you your own shade of blue.

Buried in Strange Soil

I discover a British cemetery close to my new apartment. It dates from 1854 and was originally built to bury British citizens who, not being Catholic, couldn't be interred in the local churches. It's wedged between a main road and the Manzanares, Madrid's trickle of a river, and hidden behind a high, red wall. It's peaceful and pretty, as graveyards tend to be. When the good weather arrives, I start going there at the weekends to read. One headstone — my favourite — has a misspelled epitaph. It reads: *In Lovin Memori*, the orthographical errors a reminder that the woman beneath died far from those that shared her native tongue. I wonder if foreignness is more, or less, keenly felt in a place like this. Given that, though buried in strange soil under misspelt headstones, the inhabitants have since been rewarded with the borderless heavens, where such distinctions no longer hold any meaning. Sitting there, I read a definition of belonging that suggests it lies in the answers to the following questions:

> *Who do you love?*
> *What can you leave behind?*
> *What do you need to hold on to?*
> *Where does your heart feel full?*

One Saturday morning, I wake up with nothing much to do. I feel the expansiveness of the weekend, time itself, stretching out before me. I make coffee and drink it on the terrace. The cat rolls himself around in the dust beneath my chair and I listen to the conversations of my neighbours billowing up from the apartments below. Until now, I wouldn't have been able to do that, it would have all just been noise. The heat is building along with the day and, as well as the conversations, I can hear the *tickatickaticka* of people fanning themselves next to their open windows. I stay until it gets too warm, then retreat indoors, back under the eaves.

That evening, Mum calls and asks how I am. I say: 'Good. Happy.' And then realise that I might really mean it. Later, I meet Audrey and Natalia for an ice cream. It's already 10 at night when we meet and still hot out. People are starting to appear on the street after long afternoon naps and evening showers to enjoy the relative cool of the evening, and to *paseo* through the city. The men's shirts are clean and crisp, and they smell like Álvaro Gómez cologne. The terraces of the bars are filling up, the noise is building. Natalia, Audrey and I stand in Plaza Chueca like one of those bad jokes: a Venezuelan born in Argentina, a French-Canadian, and me. The ice cream is cold and soft and sweet. I see some people I know and raise a sticky hand in greeting. When I get home a few hours later, the cat is waiting for me, having — for reasons known only to himself — forsaken his own evening paseo. I get into bed. A slight breeze cuts through the heat every now and then. He curls up in the crook of my legs, and we stay that way until morning.

> *Who do you love?*
> *What can you leave behind?*
> *What do you need to hold on to?*
> *Where does your heart feel full?*

Although it should have long been obvious, it's only now I realise that feeling like you don't belong doesn't necessarily and helpfully manifest in an opposite but related feeling that allows for a sense of belonging within that non-belonging. It can also manifest in straight-forward, heartbreaking loneliness that glues itself to you like a sticky, stinking mud. And it can do so even if you never left the estate where you were born. How might Aunty Pauline have answered those questions?

Perhaps:

> *No-one*
> *Everything*
> *Nothing*
> *Nowhere*

On my next visit to the cemetery, I notice for the first time a wall of remembrance, tucked away in a corner by the entrance. It's still in its infancy, with just a few plaques scattered at random here and there. I find the caretaker and ask about purchasing a space.

The telephone call from the cemetery secretary catches me un-aware as I'm walking the streets of the city with R. The voice on the other end of the line explains the process to me. I'm nervous of mentioning suicide, having the idea that it still constitutes dying in sin, but I'm assured that the graveyard is an inclusive place. Then, this far away, female voice asks me about my aunty, about what she was like, a question I hadn't been expecting. In turn we talk about her own aunt, whom she had been close to, and we find that our aunties had a lot in common. Her voice is soothing, never anxious or faltering (as I know my own is). She doesn't rush to end the conversation and we talk for over half an hour, two strangers, as I traipse Madrid's beautiful streets at random, R's hand in mine, his new watch strap rubbing the delicate skin on the back of my wrist. From time to time I cry, and she — this stranger — is kind. She tells me I can call about the plaque any time.

In the end, I don't buy one. It's too expensive.

Before Amy left Madrid to move back to the UK, she travelled back and forth to London for work, and sometimes I would go with her. On one of these trips, we met at Liverpool Street to catch the train to Stansted Airport. Amy was four months pregnant and serene against the chaos of the surrounding city. The train was packed; the previous two had been cancelled. From inside the carriage we watched as a woman, rushing to board, suddenly lost grip on her phone. It slid gracefully under the train and onto the tracks. She stood on the platform staring at it. The strangeness of it having just a moment before been in her hand, and it now being totally out of her reach. When we creaked out of the station, we got stuck behind another, slower train and crawled towards the airport. Squashed together, people and suitcases everywhere, everyone's eyes were on the time. At Stansted, there was a mass exodus. I lost Amy in the duty-free shop, which we were maddeningly forced to transit through. We caught each other's eye through the sea of bodies, perfume, Toblerone, luggage, and she shouted to me to run ahead and try to hold the flight. At the gate, I saw her, small in the distance, shoes off, running towards me as best she could with her bags, and the baby tucked high into her body. The woman checking my passport glanced up at Amy indifferently and then back at me, shrugging: 'If she makes it, she makes it.'

A Heartbreakingly Beautiful Setting for Saying Goodbye

I love Madrid.

I do.

And I do not regret moving.

However, I do also tend to romanticise the city and the experience of emigration in general. (And I don't regret that either.) Which is to say: there are things I wish had turned out differently, or at least that I could have found a way to interleave more elegantly — one life, one world, with the other. A rose without the accompanying thorn. Like my middle name in Spanish: *rosa linda*. In English, without the 'a' — just Rosalind, the beauty extinguished. But, a rose is a rose is a rose all the same.

At the airport, two days after my 34th birthday, my sister and I ascended the escalators towards departures. I looked down to where our parents and my boyfriend of nine years were waving us off. Tears streamed, horrifyingly, down B's face. I loved him very much, and felt so close to him that I no longer remembered where I ended and he began. Despite our terrific closeness, he wasn't moving to Madrid with me, and neither did I want him to. This other desire — to make a legitimate outsider of myself — outdated him.

After a few weeks, when I was mostly settled in, B came to visit. We sat in the walled rose garden at the bottom of the plaza where I lived without him. A heartbreakingly beautiful setting for saying goodbye. We had long been each other's best friend so there wasn't really a lot to say, we already understood how the other was feeling. He couldn't leave, and I couldn't stay. I left him to tie up the loose ends of our life together and he did so without complaint. Later, our conversation in the rose garden would come back to me in big, desperate billows of regret — on his birthday, in spring, and our anniversary, in autumn. I wondered then whether this emigration, this entire experience, only served to show me that I'd failed to understand life's most obvious and salient point: that love is the only thing that matters. That's how you know where you belong — in a place beyond place. And so, if you find a soulmate, you shouldn't toss them out of your life so easily. But that knowledge was forced on me afterwards, and by then, I was deep into the project of becoming my own soulmate instead.

In that same rose garden, four years later, I stood taking pictures of my sister and my best friend, who was visiting for a few days. They were both pregnant and we messed around taking photos of their matching bumps. My niece was born a few months after, in the bathroom of the apartment that my sister and I shared when we first moved to Madrid. Once she was a year old, and my sister was working again, they moved back to the UK for good. I've only seen my best friend's little boy a handful of times. I've missed both of their childhoods — slowly becoming a foreigner to them, a ghostlike presence popping up in conversation, though rarely in real life. And I've missed seeing, and being part of, two of the most important people in my life becoming parents.

My own parents ended up in Spain because their motorbike broke down. The summer of 2016 was a particularly dismal one in the UK, so they took a trip. Escaping outwards from home had always served to break them loose from whatever they felt was tethering them. When they had decided to reunite after a five-year separation, they had done so during a road trip through Italy on an old Suzuki GSX. This time, they rode through France, over the Pyrenees into Spain, down to visit my sister and me in Madrid, then onwards to the coast. An hour outside of Alicante, their Ducati glided calmly to a halt. The breakdown cover got them as far as the nearest dealership, but the part that was needed to fix the bike was hard to come by, and neither was anyone in much of a rush to do anything about it, given that it was the height of the hot, humid summer and a lot of businesses were closed. It took nine weeks to get Mum and Dad back on the road, by which time they had already started to look at houses. They have lived in the southeast of Spain ever since.

I often wonder, usually in that quiet moment just after waking, how much I am to blame for the anguish and isolation Mum felt in the years that followed my parents' emigration, as it was only mine and my sister's decision to move which prompted theirs. In the early years, when my sister and I were falling in love with a people and a place, when everything was so new and exciting, we barely paid any attention to our mum and dad. It was as if we didn't recognise each other anymore, as if each of us belonged to a different, distant life.

Last New Year's Eve, at my parents' house, the one they eventually bought, a neighbour knocked at the door. Conchi handed Mum a plastic bag full of oranges from her smallholding outside of town.

Mum shouted me over, to translate. Spanish is a constant source of anguish for her. Mum is a verbal person, a thinker-out loud and despite many hours of Spanish classes she still struggles. It frustrates and suffocates her, it also shames her. Conchi said to me, 'Your mum still can't have a conversation with me, after all this time. It's astounding.' I looked down to where the plastic bag was cutting into Mum's hand, turning her fingers white. Conchi didn't say it with malice, she truly did find it astounding. Perhaps it is, but she only speaks one language, one which she learnt before she was even aware of it, so really, she should have kept her astonishment to herself. When we closed the door, I took the bag from Mum and she said to me, 'She said something about me not being able to speak Spanish, didn't she?' Some things don't require translation, lying beyond language. But no easier for being so: the look on Mum's face broke my heart.

These echoes – shall we call them love's ghosts? — make their presence felt from time to time. Like when the sweet coconut smell of my sister's hair wafts past me in the street, billowing forth from a stranger's curls, or someone mentions how lush the UK is in the spring, telling me without telling me that it's no longer my home, or I catch that look in Mum's eyes which shows me she feels deeply and awfully alone. But, although there is much to regret, I know I would have regretted more not living in a way that has allowed me to try and find a place to belong, and what conditions I need to flourish. Living just once, we have to attempt whatever it is that feels imperative to us. Because if there is anything worth lamenting in the world, it is living in such a way that denies us just that.

If Self Is a Location, So Is Love

About halfway between Madrid and the coast of Alicante is a motorway service station that sells miguelitos from the nearby village of La Roda. Miguelitos are small puff pastries filled with cream and suffocated beneath a heavy dust of icing sugar. They are a staple for the holidaying *madrileño* escaping beachward. A half-forgotten box of miguelitos can be found in any office kitchen, or anywhere else polite interactions are called for. I've always associated the miguelito with a particular demographic, a particular type of person. Probably because of who I was with when I first laid eyes on one.

Carlos, V's new colleague, picked us up in Torrejón, an ugly suburb of Madrid known for its US air base and stock of starter homes. He had kindly offered to drive us to Alicante where V, his other colleagues and I were going to spend a week at the beach. We went in convoy with another car and stopped at the halfway point for lunch. There was much talk about the miguelitos and a plan was made to bulk-buy a few boxes on the way home to take to the office. (Told you.)

V had rented an apartment in Gran Alacant, a gigantic über-urb whose lateral border stretched for a distance of around eight miles. The shops and bars that popped up at random in amongst the rows and rows of identical housing were divided by the nationalities of the people living there. The urb contained worlds within a world: a German beerhouse on one side of the road stood in front of an English pub; the Swedish flag flew outside a convenience store, a block further down: a Tesco supermarket. It was impossible to know where the centre was or if there even was one. The maze-like arrangement was hypnotic and dulling. Each time V and I tried to walk anywhere we ended up lost. His colleagues were in an apartment near the beach, in a swishy resort where the Spaniards stayed. It was a long, hot climb up the hill from their accommodation to ours, the landscape getting sadder and wilder the nearer to the urb we got.

I found his colleagues boring. All they talked about was work, and they did the same thing every day: beach, three-hour lunch, nap, an evening walk and an ice cream. No deviations from this schedule were considered. I would have been happy not to see them at all. All I was interested in was V's attention. When I managed to convince him to spend the day by the shared pool near our apartment, just the two of us — away from native accents and summer schedules — I was ecstatic. But he spent the day agitatedly wondering what his colleagues were up to without him. I didn't know him well enough then to know that such uncomfortable, fidgety dissatisfaction was a constant for him. At that point, I still thought I could make him happy. We'd only been seeing each other for four months, but already cracks were starting to show. I lived for the moments when I held his gaze. And the longer there was between them, the more I unravelled.

At various points during the holiday, the plan to stop for miguelitos on the way home was discussed and reconfirmed. Now whenever I see one or hear one mentioned, I conjure again the strange parallel world of the urb, my desperation and unhappiness. And I see those people, who stood for a Spain I didn't feel associated with or connected to.

I still have never eaten a miguelito.

And then suddenly this — another Spain, another self:

R and I descend from the packed streets around the Sunday market into a dark basement club. The club is hosting an afternoon gig by Miguélez.

I say to R:
'Last time I was here, I was kissing an English bloke who was on holiday in Madrid. Over there. On the dance floor.'

He says to me:
'Last time I was here, I was breaking up with someone. Over there. In that corner.'

We aren't looking at each other, but I feel we have the same kind of look on our faces as we think about those past versions of ourselves. Something, perhaps, between distaste and indulgence. Not unlike how I imagine my face might look if I were ever to eat a miguelito.

I say:
'Maybe it was the same night.'

More to myself than to R, romantically thinking of how our eyes may have met as we queued up at the bar. Until I remembered how unromantic that actually would have been, as I hung drunkenly off the arm of a stranger and R in the process of prising a different arm from his own.

Miguélez is Luis Miguélez: guitarist, composer and front man of Miguélez, the band. And former member of the group Alaska y Dinarama, one of the representatives of the sounds and fashions of the Movida, the post-dictatorship cultural explosion in Spain. The Movida represented a new way to live, free from the constraints of the dictatorship — the cage door was open. According to R, anyone famous in the Movida doesn't like to be stereotyped by words associated with it. Words like: subversive, transgressive or counter-cultural. But they suit me because it draws a line between a life of miguelitos and a life of Miguélez. And I now know which line I belong behind.

I didn't think much about identity and plurality before I emigrated, how there isn't only a before and an after, or a this or that. Instead, all iterations of self blend in and through one another. Paint through water. In that pre-emigration view of Spain there was just one template to slot into, the one that was me there, not here. And, in the same way there was just one Spain: a place that was different to the one I was living in at the time. I've since learnt that not belonging is also a shade of the spectrum of belonging. So, it makes sense, now, that I would be drawn to the less conventional iteration of a place.

That holiday, bookended by miguelitos, feels far away in the deep past now. Blessings upon life's way of forcing change and growth in such a way that led me to a dark basement on a sunny Sunday, with Miguélez and his libertine songs of excess, my arm through the arm of someone who, this time, I truly loved.

They are extending the platform at Chamartin. The v-shaped columns that will support the metal awnings are naked for now, a cluster of concrete palm trees. Further back, other tracks have been left fallow, grass peering up between them like waterweeds, reminding me of Coventry's abandoned canals. There is new graffiti too, plastered across a broken down, double-decker train — the kind you don't see circulating very often. Ron's Crew, again urging me to 'Remember Our Name'. The railways seem to have a secret life, one where things appear overnight, made in the darkness between days, and a private language of numbers and letters — ciphers that mean nothing to me no matter how long I stare at them.

Silvia

1

There's a man outside, on the street below my window. Well-dressed, young and handsome. He is shouting: 'Silvia! Silvia!' Letting the last 'a' drag and pushing his hands desperately towards the pavement. I think (romantically) that this Silvia is a lucky woman. He has lost her and he simply cannot bear it. It's impossible for his life to continue as it once had because now there is a before and after Silvia. I keep watching him, pacing back and forth in front of a shuttered-up bar. Suddenly, he crouches down and this time his arms stretch forward, the tone of *Silvia* changes from anguished to joyous. She is a Disney cartoon of a dog, lolloping towards him, happy to have snatched an hour or so of wild freedom, but equally happy to be back in his arms. I think: *I want a man like that.*

A broken heart in November is nothing but terrible clichés. The dim autumnal days do everything they can to encourage me to feel sorry for myself. Incubating thoughts like: and what of death? Little ones, like leaves falling from trees, crunched under foot, and more substantial ones, like my own. I remember when this kind of misery felt much more thrilling and third person. Mum calls to ask what plans I have that week. I mention one or two things without much enthusiasm: 'It's something to do, you know.' She answers: 'Yes… yes. Well, that's all anything is really.' I'm not sure if this is comforting or not.

Carmen catches the waiter's eye, makes the sign that means 'two more please' and then looks at her hands, which are now gripping the empty beer bottle in front of her. She is going through a break-up too. All around us there is noisy life happening. We seem to be the only two people in Madrid who are disconnected from the collective good humour. Neither are we together in our misery, instead we are each hunkered down in our private grief. Carmen says: 'No matter how hard everything is right now, it's not as hard as losing my mother. And…' She pauses, looks at a point just past my right shoulder for a moment, then down again. 'And… Maybe this sounds clichéd, and definitely not cheerful, but I watched her die and I saw how hard she fought to stay here. When I'm feeling very low, I think of that.'

There is an etymologist on the radio, talking about ghost words. Words that, for one reason or another, made their way into the dictionary under false pretences. Misunderstandings, misspellings, oversights — it can take years to detect and eliminate them, he explains. A ghost word: the idea of an idea misinterpreted and propagated over the years, before what was there all along – what was already threaded through the very word itself – manifests, and so is erased. That was us.

Sometimes the pain will ease, its constancy abating, like the beginning of the end of hangover nausea. It's a source of hope, but I can't trust it. I'm not out of the woods yet. One cold Saturday morning, looking out at the city from my window, I see Silvia pass by. She is with a herd of other dogs — an excited, furry mass at the end of many tangled leads — being marched down the street by a stout woman wearing a Santa hat. Their collective breath clouds up towards me. I wonder where the handsome man is and why he has entrusted Silvia to this stranger, so soon after losing her. The shock and distress of not having her must have already been erased by the mundanity of having her back.

No matter how common or how communal the life experience, we can't ever fully feel the retching of another's grief, the sweep of their victories. To live through a broken heart is so universal as to have become a cliché in itself, yet it remains intensely, painfully personal. Despite the kindness lying behind the words of comfort I'm offered, and despite many of them having been won by hard experience, I doubt anyone really knows how I feel.

The ghost words are haunting me, connecting seemingly disparate thoughts and memories. Like: a trip I took to Pittsburgh, shortly after we met. I wandered around the bohemian area of that decaying, post-industrial city, which reminded me a lot of the city I grew up in. Except, here I didn't know the lay of the land, the private language of the place. I was attracted by some brightly coloured neon lights covering a shop window, announcing beer brands from all over the world. I imagined it must be some kind of craft-beer specialist, but on entering realised that it was a meeting point for local alcoholics. The shop was sparsely stocked — just enough to maintain the fiction that this was a place where people bought their essential items on the way home from an industrious day at work — and the main attraction was an area in the corner with some seats and a small boxy television, high up on the wall, showing wrestling. Customers were able to buy beer by the litre, straight from a keg. Not really knowing what to do now that I had entered under false pretences, I asked the woman serving for a beer that was locally made. She was confused by this stipulation, but like everyone else in the bar — all of whom had turned to observe me — she looked me over indulgently, understanding my misapprehension better than I did. When I told this story to a native of the city, they laughed for a full minute before explaining that what I had ended up drinking, thinking it was artisanal, was the equivalent of moonshine. That, too, was us.

An older man with crutches gets on the metro. Everyone is very solicitous and makes space for him to sit down, his broken leg becoming a collective injury to tend to. As we pull away from the station and enter the darkness of the tunnel, for no reason – or perhaps for every reason there is — the man starts to sing in a powerful, belting voice: 'I always fall in love with people that don't love me. To love this way is to die, over and over again. I can't take any more. I can't take any more.' Those that previously tended to him look away awkwardly. Someone tries to give him some money, but he pushes their hand away, further saddened by the offering.

The fashion and beauty magazines piled beside the sofa in the therapist's waiting area depress me and make me feel ugly. I think she could have made a better choice of reading materials for her clientele. A tall and graceful older woman exits the therapist's room. I look her over surreptitiously. *What can she possibly be sad about?* I think. Our eyes meet briefly and I get the feeling that she is thinking the same thing about me. I'm everyone, and no-one.

So ordinary in my huge and stupid sadness that there are no words for it that haven't already been used a million times before.

I rebel against the explanations, although I desperately seek them. What I really want is for my version of our story to be ratified by the therapist. I don't want to know the clinical analysis of us. I don't want him to be reduced to a type, even less to a disorder — for my life before him, with him, and now, to become order/disorder/order-restored. My own narrative is much more transgressive. *Let me have it, it comforts me*, I say to the therapist telepathically. I talk to him that way too. In fact, the weeks after he left have been full of some of our best and warmest conversations. I ask him now, *what do you reckon to all these theories then? Kind of easy, aren't they?* I kiss the tip of his nose, my hands in his hair. He smiles down at me, *you are my everything*. The therapist interprets my silence as reflexion.

Early on, I removed everything from our apartment that reminded me of him. Except the cat. Who is actually the biggest reminder of all. He has become uncharacteristically clingy, taking every opportunity he can to wind himself around my ankles, overeating and trilling plaintively if I leave a room, and his field of vision. However, I know that if he were to find a new home, in not much time I would be removed from his sensory memory, someone else's ankles becoming mine, mine becoming theirs. This is what everyone is telling me about heartbreak too. Clichéd, I suppose (reluctantly, moodily) because it's true: in time the pain will lessen, in time he won't matter to me. I know that at some point or another I must have said something similar to someone else, and on some level the message reaches me. But time takes all the time it wants, extending way past the reaches of my imagination, and the now of this thing is that I can't take it a moment longer. I want him to come home, I don't want to wind myself around a same but different pair of ankles.

Outside my local supermarket – the one I used to think of as *our* supermarket — I hand the homeless woman the oranges she asked me to buy her. She says thank you and I nod, not feeling up to conversation. Then, as I'm walking away, she adds: 'I love you'. Carmen was right, life makes it hard for you to give up on it, even when you really want to.

Miriam — who works with traumatised children of immigrant parents — gives me her analysis: 'He was very manipulative, but that had been his way of surviving, it was what he had become used to. Although of course that doesn't mean it's something *you* should have to get used to. It's not an excuse.' I consider this. Miriam adds: 'At some point you have to start to work through the trauma and stop living it.' I'm not sure whether she is referring to him, or me.

This is how it finally ended: I went to a party. A work party with a free bar. We had argued badly during the day and I'd asked him to spend the night elsewhere, I needed some time to think. At the party I felt by turns elated and terrified. I drank a lot and talked too much. I danced with a friend's boyfriend our bodies meeting at the points where they shouldn't meet. A colleague tried to kiss me and I almost reciprocated, not because I particularly wanted to, but because I wanted to believe I could be reborn that easily. Finally, a friend took me home in a taxi, I told him what was probably happening, I cried and he stroked the back of my hand. The taxi dropped me off in Puerta del Sol, Spain's kilometre zero, beautiful in the near dark, emptied of people. At home, I found him asleep, awkwardly, on the sofa. I put a blanket over him and went to bed. A few hours later I heard him walking around, but was unable to move for fear that we had really done it this time. So many times we had reached this point, but retreated. Eventually, I got up. I appeared in the bedroom door at the same moment that he arrived at the door to the living room. We looked at each other from opposite ends of the hallway and a long moment passed before we crashed into a hug at the mid-point. The only time in a long while we had been so in sync. Then: sitting on the end of the bed, crying. He is packing. When he is done he comes and stands over me. Puts his hand on the crown of my head. I look up at him. What did I look like to him in that moment? I tried to smile and then looked down again, unable to. He kissed me on the top of my head and left. Minutes later he came back, his tears ridiculous, pouring, mixing with snot. I stood up and we cried in each other's arms. Professions of love, etc. He leaves again. I stand in the doorway. He orders me away. *I can't watch you watching me leave.* Front door closes. A sinking to the floor. Clichés, nothing but terrible clichés.

In January, I travel to the south of Spain to visit my sister and my parents. My sister's husband is Venezuelan and his family are also visiting. We go to the beach, and when everyone takes my niece to paddle by the shoreline, I am left with Ramón, my sister's father-in-law. Whereas most people are tactfully trying to ignore my pale, ghostly face and general air of vacancy, as soon as the rest of the family are out of earshot, Ramón says to me: 'So, I hear you have a broken heart.' I'm taken aback, but appreciative – as ever — of the opportunity to talk about it. I tell him the one thing that still astonishes me, that I still cannot fathom, is how it can hurt as much as it does, or feel so much like a death. He replies: 'That's wonderful because it means you are alive.' This strikes me as cruel and essentially meaningless, but he goes on to tell me about a word used in Venezuela to describe exactly these feelings of unending misery and confusion. The word — *enguayabáo* — Ramón thinks comes from another, similar word for a tree that has twisting, gnarly roots that penetrate the ground apparently without end, impossible to ever disentangle. He also tells me that there is a type of bird that likes to nest in these trees. If the birds are sick or distressed, they refuse to leave the tree and will cry endlessly until the affliction passes and they resume their normal life. The sound drives people crazy.

I wanted to save him. I spent a lot of time trying to. Trauma, borderline personality disorder — they make you push away the very things you want the most. Self-sabotage, unpredictable behaviour, large and frightening anger, chronic insomnia, terrible fear; these things shaped his every day. When we started out, he warned me, in his way. He told me: 'I'm a very strange and difficult person and I hope you will love me anyway.' It sounded romantic! Easy to love someone no matter what when the no matter what has yet to show its face.

A friend has taken me out to eat in a restaurant. She told me to get out of my pyjamas and dress nicely. We are trying to have a nice time but I can't eat anything. My friend is impatient, and we end up sitting in silence because what else is there to do when you can't make each other happy. I excuse myself to go to the bathroom and when I come back, I find she is chatting to a couple on the next table. Tourists. They are telling her that they choose their holiday destinations based on restaurants that they want to visit. I hate them, these two and their simple, ordinary happiness. I think: *that should be us*. I pretend to read the menu to avoid having to talk to them. It couldn't be us, I realise then, just as if it were written in huge letters on the menu itself, because there was nothing simple or ordinary about him. When you suddenly understand a fact as basic as that, what is left? Only to let hope die so that something else can grow in its place.

2

'Heartbreak ought to have its own category in the *Diagnostic and Statistical Manual of Mental Disorders*.' A psychologist said that to me. He was talking about something and someone else, but it resonated. Once the sharpness of the pain had subsided and there was enough distance to be analytical, that's exactly what it felt like: recovery from a disorder. And an addiction — to the pain, the high drama, all that adrenaline that had felt like love. Now instead the calm, the sifting through. Putting everything in order so as to be able to recount the resulting thesis; the private finally becoming public and moving us into the past tense.

All my life the idea of intense experience had been romantic to me. The middle way had never held much appeal. A life of sensible qualities, a life without intensity, seemed uncool, pointless. But now I read Rilke:
Let everything happen to you: beauty and terror.
Just keep going.

And I want things to stop happening to me. I no longer want to probe the limits of my longing.

I wonder, if we had shared a homeland, would things have been different. Turkish people always liked him a lot, immediately, implicitly. This wasn't always the case with the people we met in Madrid, or anywhere else for that matter. One evening, I'm watching a television series without much interest until a Turkish character is introduced. Another character asks, 'why don't you like him?' And the reason given is not given in words, but with a gesture. He is: a sharp upwards movement of the chin and a facial expression of smelling something very bad, which I take to mean arrogant. It's the first time I have been made aware of this particular stereotype. The actor has the exact same nose I fell in love with. He had told me about this. *If you went to Turkey, you would see a million noses like mine in the first ten minutes.* Seeing this actor makes those words true — he wasn't so special. And that comforts me. What is more comforting still, is that he knew it before I did.

A sign of recovery: your story starts to become just one more of many. Reduced to a sad shrug (your own) and ready to be recycled into a cautionary tale for the next person that needs it, and there will always be a next person. Let our story get mulched up with the rest, captured by cliché, no longer mine and his, but everyone's. I am starting — thank God — not to care.

I still listen to love songs and break-up songs (some lyrics I have memorised in their entirety), talk to him in my head, fetishise the past, miss him terribly. But I also: look at other men and feel desire, luxuriate in the freedom of waking up alone. Moreover, the freedom of waking up and not waiting to see what shape his illness will take that day, which impossible question he will be asking of himself and what he will ask of me that I can't deliver. My hand doesn't slide tentatively across the bed towards him, isn't forced to make a lonely journey back to my side, I don't have to consider all the possible reasons why he doesn't want to make love. I don't have to measure up in any way. I'm enough for me. The daily rising of this intense relief is intoxicating and exciting. Like love.

Another sign of recovery: people don't want to hear about it anymore. Before, when the outpouring of emotion was beyond any kind of rational control, caring or even noticing if anyone was listening wasn't particularly important. What was important was to externalise, to purge. Now it's impossible not to notice the eyes wandering to the next table, or looking out of the window into the world — into a world where people don't bore you with their heartache. We all fail others with our lack of empathy. Or maybe it's more that we lack imagination, so impossible as it seems to be to put ourselves in someone else's shoes. Even when, at some point or another, those shoes were our own. That forever uneasy relationship between 'I' and 'you'. I try, but this still feels like the biggest thing in my life and it's hard to get interested in anything else. So, it's my failure too.

The first time I sleep with someone else I feel nothing and *this* feels like a huge achievement.

I am having a drink with three women considerably younger than me. One of them has just come to the end of a relationship. The other two rush to reassure her every time its particular shadow passes over her face: *It was mutual / It was more your idea than his*, etc. She agrees with a nod, yes, she chose this. But her face tells a different story. She looks like any typical broken heart; she looks like someone she liked very much just rejected her and that her heart is all swollen up with the pain of it. Considering my own bruised and swollen heart, I should feel a great amount of empathy for this young woman. I should remember that heartbreak doesn't operate on any hierarchy, but instead I look at her and think, *idiot*. Much in the same way as — I remember now — when I was 17 and breaking up with my first serious boyfriend. I sat in the driver's seat of my dad's car (which I had borrowed for the occasion) and felt incredibly annoyed with the snivelling teenager who had wedged himself in the opening of the car door to prevent me from leaving. I just couldn't credit his feelings, the same way I can't with this young woman. But — of course! — I'm also *idiot*, I have also wedged myself between meta-phorical car doors, I've also pretended I had agency when I clearly didn't. Despite everything, it's as hard for me as it is for anyone else to remember that 'I is [also] another'.

That day at the beach, my sister's father-in-law told me about a story by Gabriel García Marquéz called 'El olor de la guayaba' — the scent of the tree from which the name for heartbreak comes. The scent of heartbreak. I've never seen or smelt this tree, but the idea makes sense to me. Something that wafts in, sometimes sweeps in, to accost heart and mind. Just a hint of it passing quickly through the air in front of my face when I see someone across the street that looks like him, or if I'm told how stunning Istanbul is, how warm the people are. The scent will flurry and settle in various and unexpected moments. It won't take my breath away, not anymore, but it will revisit from time to time, and I will still wish that I could tell him this. That wish fed by the memory of those times when our conversations would take a turn in such way that I could almost be convinced that our being together wasn't just the result of chemicals or loneliness; that it was something more private, particular, ancient than that. A thing with unending roots.

3

Something has changed without me fully being aware of it. Men are looking at me again. Friends are introducing me to people in a way that isn't altogether casual. One of these people catches and keeps my attention. He drinks a lot, seems troubled in some murky, unspecified way. Another is kind and attentive and I am much less interested by him than I am by the sad drunk who takes to calling me at all times of the night. One morning I wake up to 17 missed calls and a stream of desperate, accusing messages. I sense the ridiculous way history is repeating itself, so I retreat back into my own company and decamp to my parents' house for the summer months. I spend time sitting, looking out at the sea, eyes hidden by sunglasses — but still vigilant — hair fat with the humidity, a golden tint starting to creep over on my skin, enjoying the sensuousness of my own company.

In the deep of summer, on my 40th birthday, I find myself night swimming in the Mediterranean with a friend. The year before, I had spent my birthday at home, drinking beer on the sofa and staring blindly at the television. I had been signed off sick from work with anxiety. His illnesses becoming mine, mine becoming his. The water is beautifully warm. The moonlight on my skin makes it shiny and iridescent, my hair – which has grown long and mane-like — drips water down my back, tacky with salt. When we finally leave, traipsing up the beach wet and happy, Audrey puts her arm around me. The sand makes her hand scratchy against my shoulder, which is a little sore from too much sun. We look at each other and smile. She kisses my cheek. *You are my everything.*

I remember reading a quote once, about love being a kind of invention, something we do to ourselves. I find it attributed to François de La Rochefoucauld. He says that people wouldn't fall in love 'if they hadn't heard love talked about'. I wonder if this way salvation lies: make the whole sad mess into a choice and thus something that we can choose to avoid. But then I listen to another break-up song and – even as I feel the sting of it still — I have to ask myself, would I really rather *live in a land where the soap won't lather?*

Back home, I open all the windows in the apartment, which is stuffy and museum-like after my summer-long absence. I let the cat out of his carrier and he sniffs the familiar, unfamiliar surroundings. There is already a feel of autumn in the air, or at least the idea of it. I peer down at the street below my window, but I don't see Silvia anywhere. Maybe she ran off again, this time for good. I notice the cat has gone back to ignoring me, in his gentle, collegiate way. And everything is quiet. For the first time in a long time.

This morning, on the train on the way to work, a busker sang Volverá, *his voice becoming distant, and then returning, as he walked up and down the aisle, a black acoustic guitar strapped to his paunch. Outside the train window, the winter sun was still rising. It's almost one year since Aunty Pauline's suicide.* Volverá. Seguro que volverá. *I know it's a love song, about the broken-hearted of a different kind, but still, the lyric, She will return. Surely, she will return, hurt.*

Mi Movida Madrileña

I always say that I moved to Madrid because I fell in love. The love I'm referring to is — as love tends to be — manifold, multifaceted and somewhat opaque. And the stories I tell about it change, depending on the day or my mood. One of them is that it all began with Pedro Almodóvar.

Like many memories, I've come to learn that this one is half-fabrication. This is a love story. Who cares about facts? I prefer my version, and I feel Pedro would agree with me.

It goes like this:

Aged 12, two years before I started studying Spanish at school, Mum, who was always interested in improving mine and Amy's minds, took us to Warwick Arts Centre, Coventry's only art house cinema, to see a film by Pedro Almodóvar. Despite the name, Warwick Arts Centre was actually located in Coventry, but — like many of the city's people and institutions — they liked to distance themselves from that fact. Although we lived on a social housing development, the arts centre wasn't that far from our home. We lived on the edge of the estate, occupying an in-between space. On two sides we were surrounded by woodland and a large open park, and on the other two by dilapidated housing and a long row of car factories. A setting which educated me perfectly in how to live in two worlds at once.

For a long time I believed that, that time when I was 12, we went to see *Todo sobre mi madre*. Although, I've since discovered that it wasn't released until seven years later. So, if we really had seen one of his films when I was 12, it would have been *Tacones lejanos* or *Kika*. And this is where I decide it doesn't matter because his films are a world of their own, and what they did, collectively and individually, was transport me.

(Later, when I started learning Spanish at school, language had the same effect. In class and instead of just mindlessly repeating, *Quiero un café solo, por favor*, I would be sitting outside, at a table shaded from the sun by a large umbrella, looking up into the face of the *camerero* and saying it. Even though my school had a bad reputation, known for its low educational standards and the troublemakers it manufactured, I was still nowhere near the top of the class, but when I heard strange words coming out of my mouth, observed myself understanding the strange words that came from my teachers' mouths, I was amazed, and could imagine that I was someone else entirely.)

Almodóvar's films represented a world that was hugely different to the one I was living in — a grey, post-industrial city, abandoned in the middle of the country, with its attitude of proud hopelessness. And people so different to me and those that I knew. Girls and women especially: the women in Almodóvar's films were bold and colourful, not timid and worried like I was. Their lives were chaotic, they didn't lay low — aim low — as I had been taught, but that was okay too, rather than something dangerous or frightening.

When I finally visited Madrid as an adult and learnt about the Movida, the cultural revolution that followed the end of Franco dictatorship and the transition to democracy, I came to understand how Madrid herself was a character in Almodóvar's films. The city represented the thrill, the creativity, the abandon of the Movida. And so, like Pedro, I fell in love with Madrid too.

When I finally emigrated, I ended up living in La Latina, the neighbourhood where many of Almodóvar's films were shot. To walk down to buy bread in the morning, I pass the fountain where, in *La flor de mi secreto*, Marisa Paredes sat and paid a man to help her yank off her boots, a present from her absent husband, which she couldn't remove by herself because they were too tight. And the apartment building where, in the final scene of *La ley del deseo*, a fire breaks out. And the serpentine backstreet where Rossy de Palma beat up Antonio Banderas for stealing her drugs in *¡Átame!*. It is like living in one of his films — an inverted reflection of when I lived in Coventry and from that distance dreamed about the world I am now living in. Walking around La Latina, I can trace a psychogeographical map of my different selves, one transposed over the other: geological layers of the self.

Watching Almodóvar's films now, decades after that first trip to Warwick Arts Centre and from the other end of emigration — from the other end of young adulthood and of the transformations both occasioned, it's like looking at a cross-section of that strata of self, and re-examining what it took for the geological layers to form. I occasionally feel the cool of a darkening shadow, a quick sweep of sadness. Perhaps because it took me so long to start to grow up and out of that proud hopelessness. But, like I said, this is a love story. And I think, in the end, it's myself that Almodóvar made me fall in love with.

Miniature Precision Components

At one time, the city centre streets were designated according to type of shop. For shoes you went to X Street, fabric Y Street. It extended to food, too. For a calamari sandwich, everybody knew that the only place to go was Z Street. Where Frank lived, this tradition remained; he lived on a street of car repair shops. When Meg went to visit him, she felt she climbed out of the metro and into the past, into a version of the city she had never known. The garages could be smelt on the approach: oil, dirt and leather interiors. It was a smell that reminded her of her father and so was uncomfortably nostalgic, but also deeply soothing.

Frank's apartment was above one of the garages. Only a few of them had living quarters, mostly they were one-story, so at night the street fell mostly quiet for lack of people. On weekday mornings, however, the screeching of the garage doors being rolled up would wake them both in a panic and moments later the air in the bedroom would be filled with the sickening, yet addictive smell of exhaust fumes.

Meg saw Frank regularly, but not so regularly as to be anything official. He was strange, similar to how she considered herself to be strange, although (unlike her) he seemed wholly unaware of this fact. Neither of them were born in that city, even in that country, and this united them in their difference. He was an engineer and fascinated by Meg's braces. "Miniature precision components" he called them, lovingly, smilingly, like it was some kind of pet name, except he would say it to her mouth, and not to her.

'And you never had braces? Or any work done?' Meg asked him on their first date. Frank's response was to bare his teeth at her. Like a snarling animal, but without aggression. More like an animal resigned to a captor. In any case, his teeth were perfect, annoyingly so; white, dainty and neatly aligned. 'No. We didn't have Dentists Without Borders where I grew up.' Then he grinned and sat back, taking a sip of his beer, waiting for her response. Meg couldn't tell if it was a joke, or even what he was trying to communicate, so the comment was just left hanging there, the first of many loose threads in their relationship. Now when they met, he always asked to see her teeth, to check how much they had moved in the intervening days or weeks between dates. He wasn't anything like Doctor Paulo, but it was quite obvious that he was some kind of connecting dot.

Meg's friend, Rocío — a native of the city — had recommended Doctor Paulo. His clinic had a strange smell and, despite all the appointments Meg had attended there over the past year, each time she entered she was struck by it. It was familiarly clinical, and so not really like a smell at all, just a smell trying not to exist, but there was something else too that she couldn't place in the beginning. Waiting for her first appointment, she had sat leafing through a catalogue of dental cutlery. It must have got into the rack by mistake, as its presence there in amongst the out-of-date gossip magazines and mangy editions of *National Geographic*, seemed menacing. For all their medical impersonality, the instruments for sale in the catalogue still looked like implements that should never be bought to use on a human body. These were tools for digging and excavating rot, and scraping and filling cavities, they seemed to belong more to a garden shed than a dentist's surgery. All the while, Meg had tried to define the smell, to put a name to it. Doctor Paulo appeared in the doorway of the waiting room calling her name, just as she got it. *Sex!* It must have been the rubber gloves, or maybe the bleach used to wash the floor, whatever it was, it was in this state of mind that she entered the consultation room, lay down in the chair, and properly looked at Doctor Paulo for the first time.

Love. Being in it, talking about it, analysing the levels of it, probing it, putting it to the test. None of it had ever sat well with Meg. It was better to divest it, make it something to stand back and observe. 'If this isn't *it*, if it all goes wrong again, then I swear I'm giving up.' Alejandra said this without grandeur, flatly, almost without sentiment. A moment passed in silence between them, these three friends who could talk for hours about love, in all its various gorgeous and maddening guises, then Rocío said, 'But even if it doesn't work out, that's not the end of love. I think it's like a searchlight, and you can chase after it, or you can wait until it settles on you, but either way it finds you in the end. That's just how it works.' Alejandra and Meg looked at each other and then at Rocío and they felt the truth of her words. Love *was* like that: ordinary people falling extraordinarily into it. They were neither special, nor blighted, they simply lay in that vast in between, like most people. Though it didn't stop fantastic things from occurring. As now, because it seemed, somehow, both like and unlike lightening, love had struck them all at the same time. And isn't that nice, whatever way you look at it?

Rocío and Alejandra had something about them. Their eyes were brighter and hair glossier, which made Meg think of a dog food commercial. The kind where the dogs come bounding out of a country house, fur lustrous and grinning an animal grin of white healthy teeth. Love was nourishing them in some way that normal alimentation could not. She wondered if she looked that way to them. They knew about Frank, but not about Doctor Paulo, and she wasn't at all sure that either relationship was particularly nutritious.

It was always a relief to re-enter the clinic. To feel the cool sting of the air conditioning, hear the squeak of plastic shoes on plastic floor, browse the dentists-recommend toothpastes and mouthwashes. Meg would feel clean again, like after the purging vomit of a hangover. She thinks Doctor Paulo's neck is her favourite part of him — can you fall in love with a neck? Separate it out from the mind it holds up and the body it connects to? Bent gently over her face, she could almost kiss it, on that soft and sensitive part near the jugular vein. He was of a dark complexion, and so his neck was a soft brown all year round. There were some stubbly hairs too, which were neatly trimmed. He had stood up and was looking at her. His masked lower face made his eyes even more present and urgent. He was asking her something, but his voice was muffled. He removed the mask and repeated: 'I was saying that I need to put a connecting band around the second molar, at the top.' He paused to ram a rubber-gloved finger into her mouth. 'Here. It's skewed out of place, and your bite is going to end up wonky if I don't. I was hoping to avoid it, but it's not possible. Is that okay?' Her mouth tasted of rubber. She looked at him, at his de-masked face, and said, 'I trust you.' And he smiled at her, and Meg thought the world could end right then and she would be perfectly happy about that.

Of course there was a precedent. When she was 15, she'd had four extractions. Her mouth was too small for all the teeth that her body was generating and the dentist needed to make space. He called it occlusion. It was the first time in her life Meg had ever heard that word, and it made her think of the section in her local library labelled The Occult. They spent hours together, her in her school uniform, prone in the chair, him peering into her mouth, right down inside of her. He was young and handsome and sweet and so of course she loved him. None of the pain that he inflicted on her could take that away and it seemed to her now that, in all the years that followed, all the various invasions on her body and mind, by doctors, artists, lovers, parents — nothing had been as intimate as those quiet hours after school was done. He had wanted her to have braces after the extractions were finished and healed, but her parents had moved them to a house on the other side of the city shortly after the work was complete and the idea just got forgotten. Until Doctor Paulo.

'I'm a very difficult person to be with.' A lot of Frank's conversations started this way. Meg was aware of some unspecified murkiness in his past, something about a bad breakup and ensuing weeks and months lost to debauchery of many different stripes, and so she had become used to his segues. 'I don't think you are particularly more difficult than most people.' She countered, calmly. He sat forward in his chair, leaning into her, challenging her with his body, but instead decided to concede the point and sat back. When he saw he couldn't ruffle her, he always relaxed. She felt that he didn't understand himself very well, that there had been a point when everything had seemed to him very black and white — as it would to an engineer — when life was simple, and he was trying to get back to that point, struggling to do so against the great and unremitting grey area of life.

'There's a club, it's not far from here actually. The whole street used to be swingers clubs and strip joints, but there's only one left now. It's all chain shops. And dentists' surgeries.' He hinted that this one last club was the one he liked to frequent, filling the conversation with the smell of leather and sweat. She wondered if he wanted to shock her, maybe even anger her, but the more unflattering details he revealed about himself, the more kindly she felt towards him. Under the table, he bobbed his left leg frantically. She kept her gaze steady and waited for him to continue. It was almost palpable, his need for acceptance, and that touched her deeply. It made Meg think of how she felt each time she sank down into Doctor Paulo's chair. The sublimation. Becoming just the sum of her parts. She was nothing but a set of teeth to him, removed from herself. But she never had felt a more intense sense of tenderness, never felt more totally exposed, than when Doctor Paulo, his face so close to hers that they might have been kissing, explored her mouth with serious intensity. When the police want to identify a dead body, which has no body left to speak of, they use dental records, so maybe that really was where her soul resided after all. Meg felt divided between her lovers, one who wanted her only for the punishments of the body, and one who only saw her soul, and denied her bodily existence.

At each monthly appointment she strained to see a wedding ring beneath his latex gloves and comforted herself with the idea that if it was there, it would be more obvious. Every now and then he would leave her alone in the chair while he went to get some new tool, or consult with one of the other dentists. She would lie there, listening to the trashy radio station he always had playing, staring up at the ceiling, and think about asking him to join her for a cup of coffee, a glass of white wine, even dinner. Maybe he liked old films, or jazz, or maybe only orthodontics interested him. She tried to think of pretexts. She was a journalist writing about dentists, she was thinking about going to dental school, she had a friend who was a journalist and was thinking of going to dental school, but she never dared. Quite aside from Freudian, or Jungian, she sometimes wondered if there was something Frankensteinian about her love for her dentist. Although she could never quite decide who was the monster and who was the doctor. He was certainly making her in his image, but then, as she had never had a conversation with him that didn't involve teeth, she was effectively doing the same. She counted the days between appointments with anticipation, but the months with anxiety, as they moved towards the date set for the removal of her braces, and so the end of their relationship.

Though the time they spent together passed easily enough, when all was said and done, Frank had never really demonstrated all that much deep interest in Meg. He was kind and solicitous, and when they made love he would stare so intently into her face that she felt paralysed, though by fear or desire she didn't know. Nevertheless, he remained somehow distant. One day, he announced he was moving to another country. She wasn't sure how she was meant to react, so she kept her mouth shut. He filled her silence with: 'We'll go together.' Of the many questions that those three words threw up (not least the fact that he had yet to tell her those other three words, nor she him), the first one to occur to her was the one that became vocalised: 'But… what about my braces? I still have six months left.' He looked at her and it seemed he really saw her for the first time. 'What a strange thing to say. You'll just find another dentist, of course.' They sat on his bed, staring at one another. A car engine sparked into life in the garage below, followed by cheering from the mechanics. Frank's eyes flickered over her face, her mouth. Carbon dioxide seeped into the room. She leaned forward and kissed him. A kiss of endings and beginnings swilling through each other, and tasting faintly metallic.

My niece was 11 days late arriving into the world. Family had gathered in Madrid to wait. At some point, I found it difficult to think of anything before or beyond this pause where life was temporarily put on hold. It was summer, so the waiting took on a languorous decadence as we passed the time in cafés and in shady plazas. After eight days of waiting, I decided to risk a visit to a friend in nearby Ciudad Real. As the train pulled out of Atocha station, Madrid disappeared to the north and ahead lay the vast, high landscape of Castilla la Mancha, Don Quijote's land — a land made for wandering and distant horizons. It was a slow crawl across La meseta and conurbations became more few and far between. The only things of interest in Ciudad Real were an abandoned outdoor cinema and a clock in the main square, which shared a certain aesthetic (carved, wooden figures creaking out of the clock face to mark the hour) with the Lady Godiva clock in Coventry. Both of which gave me an unsettling feeling of having travelled back in time, but also forwards, to some as yet unknown future. I went back to Madrid earlier than planned. I arrived home late and went straight to sleep. When I woke up, I was an aunty.

Hello, Sunshine

There was a warm day last week.

A brief spike in the temperature.

A blue sky.

I remembered a girl I overheard once, waiting to cross the road. She turned to her friend and said: *¡Huele a veranito!* The warm day last week smelt like spring burgeoning into summer, too.

It's a smell that billows out, encircling memory. Returning me to it, and it to me. I was born at the cusp of spring, and it was spring when I emigrated to Madrid — a rebirth of sorts. The whole world was flavoured by warm air then, with just a drop of minty freshness.

The bar where I ate *pan con tomate* every day for a month after I moved is now a supermarket, the fabric shop a coffee shop chain, the bakery is a holiday let. If I marked these places on a map and traced a route between them, it would make the zigzag outline of a new tulip.

The smell takes on other forms, too. It transmutes and travels where it wants. It bounces, from one ear to the other, the sound of *pipas* being split expertly between front teeth and then the crunch of the shells underfoot on Sunday nights at La Coquette. The salty taste on everyone's lips, mixing with warm beer. The house band singer's smokey voice rough with smooth undertones. The last breath of the weekend.

It grazes my lips with a first kiss. And I sense the ghost of those long, tanned fingers, enlaced through my own, their soft pressure burning a trail from fingertips to tail bone. Or the soft feel of dark curls, *remolinos*, snapping to my fingers, like the cat to my ankles after an absence.

It brings me the sun rising against a blueing sky and with it the promise of the day, one in which I try to live without cause for regret. Then later, stopping in the street, turning my face up towards it, letting it warm me, like cats do.

And its counterpart: a sunset, formidable in its splendor, triggering that blessed shiver. Memory travels through cells backwards. I'm here. I'm still here. New routes will be formed and traced eventually.

But, for a few months more, the memories must be pressed back into mothballs and cedar.

Today winter has returned, the skies are low and grey.

Redheads

Once I had a Turkish boyfriend, who assured me that there were no redheads in Turkey. Not one. He gave me *Snow* by Orhan Pamuk to read, but not *My Name Is Red* or *The Red-Haired Woman*. After we had been together for around a year and a half, and living together for a good part of that, he found out that I was not a natural redhead. Although I had never lied to him about my hair, neither had I contradicted his assumption. It was a small deception, and it seemed to make him happy. When he found out the truth, he slumped down onto the sofa, put his head in his hands and said, 'I should have known, I should have known.' Over and over again. We broke up not long after that. I don't think it was related, but you never know.

When I moved from the UK to Madrid, my hair lightened naturally with the sun, but it was still obviously brown. After a few years, my first greys started to come through and I decided to dye it. I did it at home in the bathroom at Calle de la Amnestía and instead of it coming out as my natural colour minus the grey, it somehow ended up gingery. After that, a girl at work started calling me Red. A friend, who had known me for a long time before the home-dye job, told people my hair was red because of my Irish grandmother. Another friend, who had worked as a hairdresser in her native Canada, offered to help me even out the colour. When I mentioned something about not being a natural redhead, she said, as she slapped the bright red dye onto my scalp, 'But you are really, because it's so you'.

It was frankly odd, but after a time, I started to think of myself as a redhead too.

A year after the break-up, I met someone new. My ex-hairdresser friend and I were drinking in a bar that, by chance, was adorned with illustrations of redheads. In them, everything was rendered in stark black and white, but each woman had a huge, luxurious mane of bright red hair. After the bar called time, the waiter pulled the shutters and offered us some free drinks. My friend asked what he did apart from bartending and he pointed at the drawings around us, and showed us a book he had just published called *Pelirrojas* — redheads. My friend's eyes nearly popped out of her head and she kicked me hard under the table.

Shortly after this, she got a promotion and was too busy to help me maintain the collective fiction, so I found a new hairdresser. At my first visit, after he had given me the full works and blow-dried my hair until I looked like one of the illustrations in *Pelirrojas*, I thanked him and said, 'Now my boyfriend will never know it's not natural.' He laughed, and I felt like at last I had found someone I could be sincere with. At the next appointment, he recounted the story back to me, telling me how one of his clients lies to her boyfriend, telling him that her hair is naturally red when it isn't. In the retelling it had acquired a hint of malice. However, around a year later, during some salon small talk, he asked me if I had siblings and when I said I had a sister he asked, without artifice of any kind, if my sister's hair was red like mine. It seemed there was no way of escaping my new identity.

Even though it was never my intention, I like that here in Madrid my hair stands out amongst a sea of luxurious brown and black. It's a way to flaunt my strangeness. A way that I've chosen to assume, rather than one that has been chosen for me.

99

And I still haven't told my boyfriend either.

The train pulls up to my stop. I can see the office beyond the fence that separates the station from the road. There are people – my colleagues – moving around behind the windows, starting the day. It's peaceful watching them at a remove. From this distance, everything seems to be calm and in order. I keep expecting to see myself appear through one of the doors. I'm still watching as the train pulls out of the station. I've never been beyond my stop before. I keep riding until the end of the line, where I'm forced to disembark. I cross the bridge over the tracks and wait on the opposite platform for the next train back. I'm told this kind of behaviour is typical of grief.

Saturday's Child

As canned laughter bellowed out from the television behind us, he held me. My tears wetting his jacket, which I hadn't given him time to remove. After a few minutes had passed and the juddering of my chest against his had slowed, he asked quietly: 'What happened?' I realised I hadn't explained, hadn't said anything at all, in fact, had simply opened the door to him, face already crumpled and blotchy and swollen. And he had held me.

That was the day of the second opinion.

Some years before this, a friend took me to the Prado to show me her favourite work of art, Velázquez's *Philip IV on Horseback*. We stood in front of it and I was mostly underwhelmed until she told me how, if you looked closely, you could see the horse had a fifth, painted-over leg, where the artist had changed his mind about the horse's gait and what it implied, or didn't, about the King of Spain and Portugal astride it.

I had thought about Philip IV, and the artist, so at liberty to add or remove a limb as suited his vision, as I lay on the examination table, my own legs in stirrups, looking at a framed landscape on the wall opposite. It was the kind you see in business hotels or waiting rooms. Non-places. I thought about its provenance, whether or not some-one took pride in creating it. Whether it was art or not. I didn't find it beautiful or interesting, but it was comforting me, in the sense that it was distracting me. Eventually, the doctor looked up and said: 'You know you have a tumour?' She was less asking really, more commenting, as casually as 'you know you have something in your teeth?' And as if the consequences of the two things were the same. This became the first conversation of many — held with someone's head peering up from between my legs — about the vast and complicated terrain that was my body, lying between us, both connecting and separating us.

But I didn't know him back then. We weren't friends yet.

The first time we met was in the formal setting of a classroom. We had been instructed to write our names on the folded pieces of paper provided for the purpose. Despite his name being Italian, I thought he spoke with an Irish accent. This was just one of many discrepancies: he was young, but his hair was greying. He was charming, comfortable to talk to, but something writhed beneath that smooth surface. He had no home and many homes. He seemed like an outsider too, but he was much more at ease with people than I was. He sought me out. Even though I didn't want to be. At least that's how I remember it.

At the next appointment they tell me the tumour is benign, but it has a name: fibroid. Which qualifies it as a condition. They will keep their eye on it, in case it performs some kind of trickster transformation. I don't think about it much at first. But it thinks about me, growing steadily, taking up more and more space as the years tick by. Waiting patiently for me to notice, for my mind to catch up with my body.

I get a text from a foreign number. It's him, telling me he is in town visiting a friend, and do I want to go for a drink? As I approach the corner where we arranged to meet, the midway point between the house where he is staying and my own, I see him standing with one leg resting on a yellow bollard, an elbow propped on his thigh. He looks like the lead in an old-fashioned movie. I'm nervous because the degree we are studying together makes me nervous and he is a part of that. Once we get into the bar he asks me, straight-up: 'Who do you love and who do you hate?' We get spectacularly drunk.

I don't tell anyone about the fibroid, except my parents. I think it's disgusting. I think *I'm* disgusting. Deformed. I no longer recognise myself in the mirror. I dress to hide it, I avoid swimming or being naked. It becomes an exterior thing, something on which to hang all my woes, all the second conditionals of life, each of which essentially boils down to the same thing: if only I didn't have this weighing on me, literally and otherwise, if it didn't drain me of all my self-esteem, I would soar, flourish, become another person entirely.

As the fibroid grows, stealthily and silently, so does our friendship. When he's in town, we take walks. He calls for me and I spring out of the door of my apartment building, always happy to see him, hugging him as closely as I can whilst keeping a good distance between us, between him and the hard pressure of my uterus. If only it were possible to live from the neck up; discard the clothes worn so carefully to conceal, leaving my body to sprint off, stark naked, each of us free to live apart from the other. I casually reach for the hem of his shirt to clean my sunglasses on, he smiles down at me, pretending outrage.

At each checkup I'm told to live with it, the symptoms aren't bad enough to warrant action, as if they couldn't see the swelling the size of a healthy foetus, as if that weren't symptom enough. As if I could silence my mind or blind my eyes.

Just as the fibroid has reached unprecedented proportions, I'm told I'm being discharged as an outpatient and no longer have to attend appointments at the hospital. However, their removal of me from their list doesn't dissolve the mass inside me, or the hard border I've built between me and it. I separate out our existence, making it one of mutual disdain and grudging tolerance.

We decide to take a trip. I do the four hours at the wheel and he entertains me. He tells me about an argument he has just had with a friend, the one who he visits when he's in town. Or used to. More often than not he stays with me now. He had argued that sexually explicit lyrics, as long as they were written by women, could be empowering for the artist and the listener. His friend had argued the opposite, pointing out that he wasn't in the best position to judge, given his gender. We undertake an in-depth study of all the filthiest lyrics we know, shouting them out as they come to us and playing them through the car stereo. By the time we arrive at the secluded house in the mountains we have an entirely new vocabulary, we have remapped the female anatomy, and we are drunk on laughter.

At work, I receive an email offering a free medical checkup. I make the appointment with the gynaecologist more out of a sense of responsibility than anything else. It seems like the sort of thing people are meant to do: look after their bodies. I tell the new doctor about

the fibroid as dismissively as I myself had been told about it and disappear behind the curtain to remove my clothes.

Then, there it was again: the head between my legs, telling me things
I didn't want to hear. No longer passive now though; accusing. How
could I have let myself get into such a state? Didn't I know the
danger? Or about the stress on my organs? Didn't I know I may as
well be six months pregnant? Couldn't I *see* myself?

This doctor wants me to go to the emergency room. She doesn't
think I should wait a moment longer, let alone for the menopause,
as I had been previously advised. She writes a letter to my doctor.
As she does so, the nurse takes my blood pressure. The reading is so
high they won't let me leave until I calm down. I don't calm down,
but they let me go anyway because the clinic is closing for the night.

I get home 15 minutes before he is due to arrive. I go through the
motions of finding the film we had planned to watch, switching on
the TV, putting the snacks out, tears falling constantly, fear and grief
splattering onto every surface I come into contact with. When the
doorbell rings, I open the door to him, my face already crumpled
and blotchy and swollen.

He is the first person, apart from my parents, that I tell.

I go to my doctor, brandishing the letter from the gynaecologist. If
they won't believe my experience of my body, they must believe the
version from one of their own. The new hospital agrees with the ex-
clamation mark-filled letter and I'm scheduled for surgery.

After I'm discharged, he comes over to cook for me. I lie on the sofa trying not to cough, or laugh, as they both hurt, and make me afraid of bursting my stitches. He asks me about the drugs I was given at the hospital and if I liked them. I had thought the soft, dreamy feeling was natural, a result of being restored to myself. Over lunch, I start to cry. Out of nowhere, in the middle of a sentence. 'It's the drugs.' He tells me, knowingly. He reaches out, puts his hand on top of mine, then his other hand on top of that, and leaves them there until the tears pass. The next day he come backs and makes me lunch again. This time he brings with him a stone for sharpening my knives. I lay with my eyes closed, hidden behind the back of the sofa, listening to the slicing sound of the blades getting filed, a sound both soft and strong.

The summer after the surgery he moves again, this time too far away to visit. At first, I don't notice his absence because another present absence has eclipsed him. Life feels hopeful again. I look at myself in the mirror all the time, amazed at my new/former body.

Contact between us trails off.

I feel abandoned, his absence a judgement on my relocation from mind to body. I'm touchy and easily hurt when he does contact me.

As our friendship sinks definitively into silence, I start to wonder if that hard, angry growth had been the centre that held us in equipoise. *Who do you love and who do you hate?*

In bed at night, I lay a hand on my flattened stomach. I'm reconciled to myself. I think about gains, about losses. And sometimes — as I trace the concave that now descends from my hipbone to the emptiness newly held there — I think of him.

In a Third Place

Airport (Madrid Barajas): *The view from your hotel window*

You could be anywhere: an apartment block with lights lit here and there, the dentist surgery underneath them, a cat slinking between the parked cars. A kilometre away Barajas looms, its vast empty runways marking territory in the surrounding city. Airports: you could be anywhere, yet their purpose is to take you anywhere at all in the world. There is promise in that nothingness.

You were meant to be taking this trip with a friend. The plan was to meet in Amsterdam; you travelling from Madrid and her from London. However, at the last minute she is stricken by a mysterious illness and so you go it alone.

Amsterdam — Day One: *Repeating patterns*

It seems that every city you revisit you end up retracing your steps, like some kind of tourist manifest destiny. You are landed in the central Amsterdam of six years ago (driven there by a statuesque Surinamese bus driver. He wears sunglasses despite the greyness of the day and gives a sideways, scissory peace sign to all the other bus and tram drivers that pass him). Without design or desire you are staying on the same road that you stayed on in another life, in another identity. Places and streets you didn't even know you remembered stumble into your path, eager to greet you again.

You make a new rule: it is now forbidden to do anything you have done before, even if you like doing it. You keep being drawn to these ghost places though. You spy a bar that looks cosy and inviting so you cross the street and enter it: you came here on visit one. You look left and see a pretty side street with flowers and a skinny canal that bends pleasingly to the left, so you take it. Halfway down you begin to recognise the bend: visit two.

You decide maybe it doesn't really mean anything, just that you are attracted to certain things, particular aesthetics and nothing more. It doesn't say of you that you are rigid and resistant to change. But you stick to the new rule anyway because, after all, you like rules.

Day Two: *Amsterdam inspired Haikus*

Hazy, sleepless day / The streets resonate through time / Disorient you

*Where do you belong? / Where you were born, here, or there? / Not one place, but all/none**
*delete as applicable

Wheels and water flow / Discordant with the language / Your steps fall in time

Houses with backs straight / The cobbles like sticks of gum / As the clouds look on

You find a bar which is the perfect amount full. It always used to feel more glamorous drinking alone with your well-chosen accessories (tonight, F. Scott Fitzgerald), but the truth is you get bored of your own company. Later on that evening you find the answer to this boredom: have exactly two more drinks than you intend to, then you are more than enough for yourself.

Day Three: *Walking past a shop called The Otherist you discover your -ism!* The first question people always ask here is 'where are you from?' How to respond, here in a third place? With the country you were born in, or the country you now live in? Your ear strains to hear the cadence of Spanish over your native tongue, your eyes delight to hit upon an olive-toned face which suggests warmth to you, not just because of the connotation with sunshine (which is in short supply here).

However, either way, you discover the best visa is your smile — the Esperanto of facial expressions.

Day Four: *A visit to the tulip museum*
It is the most innocuous of places yet all you can think about is sex and money. You learn that just before the tulip market crashed in the late 17th century the flowers were valued at hundreds of times over the weight of gold. The right bulb could guarantee you a couple of canal-side town houses.

There is a quote from someone called Lelezari, from the 18th century:

Curved as the form of the new Moon, her colour is well apportioned, clean, well proportioned, almond in shape, needlelike, ornamented with pleasant rays, her inner leaves as well, as they should be, her outer leaves a little open, as they should be; the white ornamented leaves are absolutely perfect. She is the chosen of the chosen.

Which sounds far too much like the description of a vagina to be a coincidence. This is taken from a piece called 'Acceptable and Beautiful'. Sex and money mulch together to become one and the same thing: power.

Breukelen — Day Five: *Somehow you find yourself in Brooklyn*
Its namesake anyway, its precedent in fact, located outside of Utrecht. Your host collects you from the train station and on the journey to the canal-side house, perfect in its symmetry, where you will be staying, he tells you that he was born in the other Brooklyn, New York. He has lived in Breukelen, the mirror, the ghost, for 50 years. He tells you a story that resonates with your own (that of falling in love with a place and a people), then pauses and adds: 'There's nothing to make you look away here.' You think what a lovely sentence that is. Then wonder: what's wrong with looking?

He and his wife are art historians and they have certainly created the pastoral idyll. You read the guest book which is stuffed full of praise, not just for the beautiful lodgings, but for the owners themselves; their kindness, their grace, their intelligence and urbanity. You had wanted to write something similar yourself until you read what those before you had said. You wish you could find new words for timeless sentiments.

Utrecht — Day Six: *The time comes to leave the idyll*

You leave as authentic a comment as you can muster in the guest book, but the truth is their grace makes you uneasy with yourself, reflexively it makes you interrogate you own flaws, but you are genuine when you speak of their warmth.

Warmth is in short supply. This will be the fourth day in a row that you have been soaked through. It doesn't seem to dampen anyone's spirits though, you guess they are used to it here, as you used to be used to it, too. You are beginning to long for Madrid, for her dry, sharp cold, a cold which is guaranteed to be followed up by a dry and infernal heat.

Airport (Amsterdam-Schiphol): *In the toilets there is a flight attendant putting on her make-up and fixing her hair*

She is tall, slim and blonde, like an air hostesses of yesteryear. A girl rushes into the bathroom and starts to rummage through the bin next to you, she says she has left part of her hen party outfit in there. She retrieves it and joins the tall blonde at the mirrors. You glance over to find that she is wearing an air hostess costume. You look at them both, the real and the pretend versions of each other, and you smile.

Once upon a time, Mum, Aunty Pauline and I went on a pilgrimage — a five-day walk in the south-east of Spain, from Orihuela to Caravaca de la Cruz. The path followed an abandoned train line. Now and then a bit of old platform would appear, the strata of the paving exposing the different eras of civic planning. Many of the stations were still standing (although their interiors were falling apart) and decorated with glossy green tiles declaring the now forgotten and irrelevant names of each stop. Part of the walk ran through an area called the Badlands, a dry, dusty landscape with odd, strangely shaped hills pushing upwards from the earth. Some old Westerns were filmed there, tricking audiences into thinking they had left Spain and materialised in the Wild West. What was she thinking then, in those years before her suicide? Was there something about the empty landscape, dogs howling in the distance, the forgotten, decrepit train line that spoke to her about the horrors of impermanence? How time escapes us no matter what, and that our ceasing to exist will only be of importance to a handful of people. I should have told her, a hundred times a day, how very far from insignificant she was to me.

Contents

Casio, 1984 — 3

Sites of Conscience and Memory — 9

Forever Falling to The Ground in A Faint — 19

Baba Ghanoush — 25

The Blessed Shiver — 31

Buried in Strange Soil — 35

A Heartbreakingly Beautiful Setting for Saying Goodbye — 43

If Self Is a Location, So Is Love — 49

Silva — 57

Mi Movida Madrileña — 75

Miniature Precision Components — 81

Hello, Sunshine — 93

Redheads — 97

Saturday's Child — 103

In a Third Place — 111

Acknowledgments

I always wondered what it would feel like to write one of these.
I'm worried about missing people out. Which I guess is what happens
when you've been writing for such a long time, when you've foisted
scribbled, fevered copies of things onto so many people over the years.

Here goes:

For having the idea to put this collection together, and for believing in
my writing, thank you to my publisher and friend, Maria Glymph,
without whom I wouldn't be writing these words at all.

And the one teacher I can say changed my life: Anna Beer.

For taking care of my heart and supporting me always and in everything:
Lynda Marshall, Gary Marshall, Amy Marshall, Julie Pate.

Mi amor: Rashid El Jaouhari.

Incredible friends who have known me for so long that they've seen me
through all and everything life throws at us, and who I love with all my
heart: my unofficial second sister, Cally Peece, Sally Rose, Sally Parker,
Vanessa Jacques, Nadia Gradecky, Adriana Alba.

Incredible friends and editors, my loves: Nikki Strutt, Susanne LaBrake.
Top of my cheerleading pyramid, friend, first reader and the proof that true,
deep connection really can leap from the screen into real life: Kay Stratton.

Absent friends who have been a huge part of my life, my love to you:
Mattia Ferrario, Brett Atkinson.

About Jayne Marshall

Jayne Marshall is from the UK but lives in Madrid, Spain. She is an editor and a fiction writer and essayist. Her work has been published in magazines and anthologies around the world, including as a nominee for the Aesthetica Creative Writing Award (UK). She holds the Master's in Creative Writing, with distinction, from the University of Oxford. She also writes a regular column for *The Madrid Review*.

Credits

In 'The Blessed Shiver' the Nabokov quote is taken from his autobiography *Speak, Memory*.

The questions about belonging in 'Buried in Strange Soil' come from Salman Rushdie's *Joseph Anton: A Memoir*.

The title 'If Self Is a Location, So Is Love' is taken from the poem 'The Aerodrome' by Seamus Heaney.

In 'Silvia', the line '…live in a land where the soap won't lather' is taken from the song "The Only One" by Billy Bragg.

'Baba Ghanoush' was first published in *Pure Slush* in 2023.

'Silva' was first published in *The Lovers Literary Journal* in 2023.

'Casio, 1984' was first published in *Prairie Schooner* in 2021.

'Miniature Precision Components' was first published in *The Rational Creature* in 2019.

About Modern Odyssey Books

Modern Odyssey Books publishes literary fiction, poetry, creative nonfiction, short story collections, and other narrative forms. In addition, Modern Odyssey produces the literature-inspired *In Search of...* puzzle book series.

We take readers on the magical and adventurous journey of words and stories.

www.modernodysseybooks.com

ISBN: 979-8-9990563-1-3

Modern Odyssey Books
Maria Glymph, Publisher
www.modernodysseybooks.com

9 798999 056313